Winnie
AND Wilbur

WINNIE'S
Alien
Sleepover

Parmar

The Little Ordinaries

Beddy-Teddy

Scruff

Jerry the Giant

To Gary and Anny for the great road trips!—K.P.
For everyone at St Paul's Primary School in Cambridge.
I'm proud to be their Patron of Reading!—xx

OXFORD
UNIVERSITY PRESS

Great Clarendon Street, Oxford OX2 6DP

Oxford University Press is a department of the University of Oxford.
It furthers the University's objective of excellence in research, scholarship,
and education by publishing worldwide. Oxford is a registered trade mark of
Oxford University Press in the UK and in certain other countries

Text © Oxford University Press 2015
Illustrations © Korky Paul 2015
The characters in this work are the original creation of Valerie Thomas
who retains copyright in the characters.

The moral rights of the author/illustrator have been asserted

Database right Oxford University Press (maker)

First published in 2015
This edition first published in 2016

British Library Cataloguing in Publication Data
Data available

ISBN: 978-0-19-274849-2 (paperback)

6 8 10 9 7 5

ISBN: 978-0-19-277817-8 (Pack)

Printed in India by Manipal Technologies Limited

Paper used in the production of this book is a natural,
recyclable product made from wood grown in sustainable forests.
The manufacturing process conforms to the environmental
regulations of the country of origin.

LAURA OWEN & KORKY PAUL

Winnie AND Wilbur

WINNIE'S
Alien
Sleepover

OXFORD
UNIVERSITY PRESS

CONTENTS

WILBUR'S
Got Talent

WINNIE'S
Alien Sleepover

WINNIE'S
Lost Teddy

Snip-snap! Snip-snap!

Winnie's alarm croc thought it was time to get up.

'What the wobble? I was as fast asleep as a cheetah!' said Winnie, waking with a start.

'Mrrow,' muttered Wilbur. He was holding on to the very edge of the bed. He hadn't slept at all well. Winnie and her teddy bear had hogged the bed all night long.

Yawn! Winnie flung her arms out wide for a morning stretch . . . punching Wilbur right out of bed—**bump!** Winnie didn't even notice what she'd done. She was hugging her teddy bear, and smiling at him. 'What a cuddly friend you are, eh, old Beddy-Teddy?'

Wilbur scowled.

Bing-bong-smelly-pong!

'Whoever can that be at the door?'
wondered Winnie, pulling on her messing

gown.

Wilbur stamped down the stairs, and—

creak!—opened the door.

'Good morning!' said Mrs Parmar,
standing on the doorstep with two little
ordinaries from school. 'We are collecting
jumble for the sale at school tomorrow.
Do you have any, well, *nice*, jumble for us,
Winnie?'

'Ooh, I'm sure I can find you some bits
and blobs,' said Winnie.

'Now, where did I put that make-your-wellies-smell-nice machine that Auntie Aggie gave me for my birthday? I've never used it, and I never will.'

'That sounds lovely!' said Mrs Parmar, sounding surprised. 'Perhaps you've also got some toys you've outgrown?'

Winnie wasn't listening. She had her head in a cupboard and her bottom in the air, searching for the make-your-wellies-smell-nice machine. But Wilbur *had* heard what Mrs Parmar said, and it gave him a very, very, very wicked idea.

Quickly, sneakily, Wilbur scuttled up the stairs and into the bedroom. He snatched Beddy-Teddy, and then slid sneakily down the bannisters.

Before Winnie's head was out of the
cupboard Wilbur popped Beddy-Teddy
into the jumble box, and stepped in front
of it to hide what he had done.

'Here it is!' said Winnie, hauling out a
huge box. 'Urgh! It smells of rosy-posies
even when it's not switched on. I'll be glad
to be rid of it.'

Wilbur stepped forward. He lifted the
box into the crate of jumble, squashing
Beddy-Teddy out of sight.

'Ooh, thank you, Wilbur; you're such
a gentleman!' said Winnie. Wilbur looked
at the floor. 'And modest with it!' said
Winnie.

14

And off went Mrs Parmar and the little
ordinaries with their box.

Winnie and Wilbur had a sort of normal
day after that, except that Wilbur kept
helping Winnie with everything.

'You're being very noble today,' said
Winnie. She didn't guess that he was
feeling very guilty about something.

15

After supper Winnie had a bath (with
Wilbur scrubbing her back), put on her
nightie and cleaned her teeth (Wilbur
had already squeezed the toothpaste for
her), and climbed into bed (Wilbur had
plumped her pillows).

'Come on, Wilbur, it's beddy-byes
time,' said Winnie.

So Wilbur jumped onto the bed too. He
lay there, stiffly, eyes wide open. There
was lots of lovely room, but Wilbur wasn't
happy . . . and, soon, neither was Winnie.

'Where's my cuddly-as-a-puddly old
Beddy-Teddy gone?' she said.

'Mrrow?' Wilbur shrugged and tried to
look innocent.

Winnie looked under the bed. She
looked in the bed. She looked around the
room. She looked around the house. She
looked around the garden.

'I can't sleep without my Beddy-
Teddy,' said Winnie. 'Oh, I'll just have to
make myself a new teddy bear.'

Winnie snipped and stitched and stuffed
some old stockings.

'Oh, no! It looks more like a snake and it's not going to give me sweet dreams!' she said, tears wobbling in her eyes.

'Meeow?' sighed Wilbur. He handed Winnie her wand.

'Of course!' said Winnie. 'Wilbur, you are not just a gentleman cat, you are also a genius! I'll magic my dear old Beddy-Teddy back.' Winnie waved her wand. '*Abracadabra!*'

Grrrowl!

There *was* a bear, but it was hairier and scarier than Beddy-Teddy used to be!

'Er, oh my, how you've grown while you've been away, Beddy-Teddy!' said Winnie. The great big bear picked Winnie up as if she was *its* toy, and then snuggled into bed—**creak!**—and went to sleep. But Winnie was wide awake!

'Mrrow!' said Wilbur. It was all his fault! Wilbur knew that he must get the *real* Beddy-Teddy back, and fast!

Wilbur snapped on a cat-burglar mask, rushed from the house, and hurried down the dark streets to the school.

Everything was dark, dark, dark . . .
except for a spark of light that flickered
inside the school! Wilbur peered. Wilbur
prowled. Wilbur prised open a window.
And Wilbur pounced . . .

Leap . . . Hiss!

Wilbur the cat burglar caught a human
burglar at work! He was clutching the
head teacher's laptop and Mrs Parmar's tin
of toffees!

'Meeow!' Wilbur told him sternly, and he bound the human burglar up. Then he used the human burglar's mobile phone to text the police—**bleep! bleep! bloop!**

Wilbur could see Beddy-Teddy on the table of toys for sale. So, quick as a flick, Wilbur grabbed Beddy-Teddy back, and he escaped out of the window, just as the police arrived.

With Beddy-Teddy held tight in his teeth, Wilbur commando-crawled past the police car, and hurried home to rescue Winnie from the bear that wasn't her Beddy-Teddy. Was Winnie still all right?

She was! The big hairy scary bear had disappeared. And Winnie was fast asleep, clutching her wand.

'Meeow!' sighed Wilbur happily. He
took off his mask and tucked Beddy-
Teddy under Winnie's arm, then he
snuggled in beside them. **Wallop!**
Winnie reached out her other arm in her
sleep, pushing Wilbur to the very edge of
the bed. But he didn't mind.

Zzzz!

In the morning, Winnie said, 'I had
a strange dream last night, Wilbur. I
dreamed that there was a *real* bear in my
bedroom. Can you imagine? And then . . .
oh, my giddy gracious me, look, Wilbur!
I've just found my old Beddy-Teddy!' And
she hugged Beddy-Teddy, and she cried
again. 'Silly me. He wasn't lost at all!'

Wilbur didn't say anything.

Down at the jumble sale, there was gossip about a burglar found all bound-up in the school the night before.

'Fancy stealing other people's things! That's as nasty as filling somebody's bed full of slugs, that is!' said Winnie.

'Mmm,' said Wilbur.

Guess what Winnie bought at the jumble sale? A funny little old teddy bear for Wilbur. So now there's even less room in their bed!

ΣΑΜΣΟΥΝΓ

WINNIE'S
Upcycled Bicycle

Crackle! went Winnie's television, and
the picture went fizzy, just when a player
from Womanchester United was about to
score a goal.

'Oi, I want to see that!' said Winnie.
She thumped the television so hard that
the whole room shook . . . bringing a black
shower of soot down the chimney.

Cough! went Winnie. **Cough-
cough-cough!** 'Oh, flapping flip-flops!'
said Winnie. 'Now I can't see a thing! I

need to clean the chimney and sort the television aerial. Where's my broom, Wilbur?'

Winnie rammed her broom up the chimney. The broom didn't like being rammed, so it wriggled and struggled, showering down soot.

'Behave yourself, Broom!' said Winnie. **Cough-cough!** 'Go on, up you go!'

And suddenly the broom did go up the chimney: fast, right out of Winnie's hands.

'Well, that's—**cough!**—shifted some of the soot!' said Winnie. 'But now my broom is right up the chimney where I can't reach it. It's blocking the chimney worse than ever! What a mess!'

'Mrrow?' said Wilbur.

'Well, I could get Jerry round to sort the
chimney, but . . .'

'Yoo-hoo, Missus!' came a voice through the window.

'Jerry!' said Winnie. 'I was just talking about you! Can you sort our chimney for us, er, but without knocking it all down, do you think?'

'Well I was goin' to go on a
bike ride while the sun is out,
Missus. Why don't you come
and 'ave some fresh air wiv me,
and we can sort the chimley
when we get back,' said Jerry. 'It's
a loverly day for a bike ride.'

So Winnie and Wilbur went out to
where Jerry and Scruff were all ready with
their bicycles.

'You is as mucky as a pup
wot's rolled in muck!' laughed

Jerry. He got onto his penny-farthing
bicycle. 'Come on, then!'

'But Wilbur and I haven't got bikes!'

said Winnie. 'Oh, but I could you-
know-what!' Winnie waved her wand.
Abracadabra!

And instantly there was a green scooter,
just like Scruff's, for Wilbur.

'Purr!'

Abracadabra! again, and instantly
there was a shiny blue bicycle for Winnie.

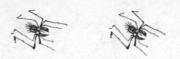

'Off we go, then!' said Jerry, and he and Scruff and Wilbur wheeled off down the road.

But—**roll-crump!**—Winnie fell straight off her bicycle.

'Oh! Cycling isn't as easy-sneezy as it looks!' said Winnie, wriggling her legs. 'Ooh, I know what to do!' Winnie waved her wand. *'Abracadabra!'*

Instantly Winnie's bicycle had
stabilizers.

'That's better! I like those,' said Winnie.
'Ooh, I could add some other bits while
I'm at it!'

While Jerry and Scruff and Wilbur
disappeared into the distance, Winnie kept
waving her wand.

'Abracadabra!'

Instantly her bicycle had a big shiny bell and a horn.

'Abracadabra!'

Instantly it had a big basket and lights.

'Abracadabra!'

Instantly it had a pair of wings.

'Abracadabra!'

Instantly it had a rocket engine.

'Ah, that's a lot better!' said Winnie, climbing onto her superbike. 'Look out, you lot, here I come!'

Zoom! Ting! Honk-honk!

Winnie's superbike whizzed along the road so fast that the soot blew off Winnie.

Soon she was catching up with Wilbur and Scruff and Jerry who had just reached the top of a hill.

But—**neeow!**—Winnie didn't stop when she reached them. She was going so fast, powered by the rocket engine, that at the top of the hill her bicycle took off!

'My bike's flying!' said Winnie. 'Whee! Er, whoopsy!' Winnie swerved to miss a tree. 'Oops, now I'm heading back towards home. Jerry! Wilbur!' Winnie called, but all Wilbur and Jerry and Scruff could do was watch Winnie whizz overhead.

40

'This bonkers bike isn't as easy to steer as a broom!' wailed Winnie. 'Oh no . . . !'

CRUMP!

Winnie crashed . . . onto the roof of her own house. Her lovely blue bicycle was crumpled around her television aerial.

'And how on Earth and Moon and Jupiter am I going to get back down to the ground now?' wondered Winnie. 'This bike isn't going to fly again.'

There *was* a way down, but it wasn't a nice or a clean way.

'I'll have to go down the chimney,' sighed Winnie, and she climbed into a big chimney pot as if she was a witchy Father Christmas with no presents.

It was dark and cramped and—**cough-cough!**—sooty in the chimney. And, as Winnie wriggled downwards, she suddenly got prickled.

Eeek! 'What the dithering doughnuts is that?' said Winnie. But she soon realized

that it
was the
bristles of
her broom,
still stuck in
the chimney.
'Right,
well you
and I had
better go
down together,
Broomy,'
said Winnie.
The chimney
got swept
as they
went.

Bump-bump!

Winnie and her broom landed back in her filthy room just as Jerry and Wilbur and Scruff rushed in, all out of breath.

'Oh,' said Jerry. 'You look like the inside of a vacuum cleaner bag, Missus!'

'Me-he-he-ow!' laughed Wilbur.

'Ruff-ruff!' agreed Scruff.

'Come outside, Missus, and I'll make you a shower,' said Jerry.

Jerry fixed his hosepipe to his big
penny-farthing wheel to make a fountain
shower.

'You're as clever as a tap-dancing
turkey, Jerry!' said Winnie. 'Ooh, this is
lovely!' She ran in and out of the water,
getting nice and clean. Wilbur sat and
washed himself the cat way.

Then, snug in her fluffy messing gown, Winnie went back inside her house.

'There's another football match to watch,' said Winnie. But then, 'Oh!' She put her hands to her cheeks. She'd forgotten how dirty her room was! 'Oh, please, dear Broomy, would you clean up our room? I'll wax your bristles afterwards!'

46

And—*swish-sweep-swish!*—

the broom gathered the sooty dust, and

binned it. It didn't get the room perfectly

clean, but it was good enough for Winnie

and Wilbur.

'Good,' said Winnie. 'Now, Jerry,
you make yourself comfy sitting on my
big trampoline, and watch through the
window. Scruff and Wilbur and I can all sit

on the big comfy sofa.'

When Winnie switched on the
television, the picture was perfect and the
sound was crystal clear.

'My bike stuck to the aerial has made all the difference!' said Winnie. 'That's much better . . . er, even if it means that I can see that Womanchester United are losing. Boo!'

'It's only a game, Missus,' said Jerry.

'You're absolutely bowl-of-fruitely right, Jerry,' said Winnie. 'And, talking of fruit, would you like a nice pickled parsnip and pongberry milkshake with a few gooseberry crisps?'

'Er, no fanks Missus,' said Jerry. 'I'm on a diet.'

Scruff was on a diet too. So Winnie and Wilbur ate and drank it all.

WILBUR'S
Got Talent

'Meow?' said Wilbur. He opened the
fridge door to reveal just one shrivelled
carrot with a furry end, a bottle of milk
that had turned to green lumps bobbing in
yellow water, and a maggot that looked at
Wilbur and winked. Wilbur shut the door.

'I'm sorry, Wilbur,' said Winnie, talking
through a mouthful of toasted gherkin
flakes. 'I didn't know there was nothing
else left. What's in the larder?'

Wilbur opened the larder door and

53

stared. The shelves were empty except for spiders' webs, and . . .

'Look!' said Winnie, peering into the gloom at the back of one shelf. 'There's a . . .'

Winnie pulled out a slightly rusty tin with 'Fogle's Fancy Nancy Food for Faddy Cats' on the label.

Wilbur stuck out his tongue and made a disgusted face.

'Oh dear,' said Winnie. 'You don't like that brand, do you? I thought I'd given all of those tins away to Wanda, but I must have missed this one. There was some competition to be the pussycat model for advertizing Fogle's Fancy Nancy wot-not, and Wanda was sure that her Wayne would win it and be a star. You had to find a golden paw print on the lid, or something, but they never found it.'

'Meeow!'

Wilbur was so hungry, he didn't care that it wasn't his favourite food. He found a tin opener, and—**Clank! Wind-wind-ping!**—up popped the lid, and an awful quite-wrong-for-food pong wafted out. Wilbur clamped a clothes peg on his nose, and dug a paw into the tin. He was about to put the pawful of awful food into his mouth when . . .

'Oh, Wilbur!' screeched Winnie, waving the tin lid. 'Look, look, look! It's a golden paw print, Wilbur. You've **won!** You're going to be a star!'

A big cheesy grin spread over Wilbur's furry face. He took the clothes peg off his nose, patted his ears into place, stroked along his whiskers, and raised one eyebrow.

Winnie pulled her mobile moan from her pocket. 'I'll ring the Fogle food people straight away! Ooh, you'll be rich, Wilbur! Famous!'

Soon a sleek limousine pulled up outside. The chauffeur opened the car door, and Wilbur stepped inside, sweeping his tail after himself.

The chauffeur was about to shut the door, but Winnie pushed her way in, too.

'I'll have you know that I am Mr Wilbur's manager,' she said, bending her hat with as much dignity as she could.

They waved at passers-by, and drank lemonade with posh straws.

'Ooh, this is the life!' said Winnie.

But she didn't think so for long. At the studio, a frilly-shrilly woman put Wilbur on a stool. She washed him and trimmed him and scented him and brushed him.

'But he hates . . .' began Winnie, before Wilbur gave her a look from the mirror that made her be quiet.

A woman with a broom swept away Wilbur's fur clippings. A man brought Wilbur a fish lolly to lick. Another man powdered Wilbur's nose, then slicked Wilbur's head hair sideways.

A man with a clipboard spoke to Wilbur. 'When you're ready, Sir, we can begin filming while you enjoy a bowl of Fogle's Fancy Nancy Food for Faddy Cats.'

60

'But Wilbur doesn't like . . .' began
Winnie.

'Erm,' interrupted the man with the
clipboard. 'Would you care to go home
now, witchy lady? We don't want Mr
Wilbur to be distracted.'

'Oh!' said Winnie. 'Well, I don't want
to embarrass you, Wilbur. Er, I'll just go
then, shall I?'

Wilbur didn't say a thing.

So Winnie went home. All on her own.
On the bus. She saw through the window a
man putting up a huge poster, of . . .

'Wilbur, my Wilbur!' said Winnie. It
was Wilbur, looking all smart beside a dish
of Fogle's Fancy Nancy Food for Faddy
Cats. 'Ooh, doesn't he look handsome?'
said Winnie to everyone on the bus. 'He's
my cat, you know!'

It's funny how you can feel happy and unhappy at the same time. Winnie felt very lonely when she got home, even though she was proud of Wilbur. And she was worried when she looked around her house.

'Oh dear,' she said. 'I don't think this place is smart enough for Wilbur now. Will he still want to live here? With me?

I'd better make it suit his new style.' So
Winnie waved her wand. *Abracadabra!'*

And instantly her house pulled itself
together, from saggy, sloppy, scruffy
comfort to something sharp and smart.
And so did Winnie.

Smart Winnie sat in a smart chair and switched on her *huge* smart television. And guess what she saw?

'Wilbur!'

There was Wilbur chewing and chewing and chewing on some Fogle's Fancy Nancy Food for Faddy Cats.

'Oh, Wilbur, I can see you don't like it!' said Winnie to the television screen. She got up. 'Oh, I can't stand this any longer. I'm coming to fetch you home, Wilbur!'

Winnie jumped on her broomstick and flew straight to the film studios, and in through an open window. She remembered the woman sweeping up Wilbur's snipped fur, so she waved her wand.

'Abracadabra!'

Instantly Winnie had a pinny on. She began sweeping with her broom, sweeping from room to room.

Sweep-sweep, through the hairdressing and make-up place, **sweep-sweep,** through the filming area, **sweep-sweep** ... and then Winnie heard a tiny pitiful,

'Miew!'

'Wilbur!'

Winnie burst through the door. There
was Wilbur, sitting in splendour but all by
himself, with an untouched bowl of pongy
Fogle's Fancy Nancy Food for Faddy Cats
in front of him.

'MEEOW!' he shouted with delight when he saw Winnie, and he leapt into her arms.

'Oh, Wilbur!'

Clack-clack, there was the sound of footsteps coming along the corridor.

'Quick!' said Winnie, and she and
Wilbur leapt onto the broom, and off they
zoomed, out through the window, just as
clipboard-man and frilly-shrilly-woman
came through the door.

Winnie and Wilbur flew home. Winnie
closed the door firmly, then she locked it.

The first thing Wilbur did was pounce
on a fat mouse.

'Oh, I'm sorry, Wilbur!' said Winnie. 'I thought I'd made everything properly smart for new smart you. That mouse must have been hiding from the magic!'

'Meeow!' smiled Wilbur.

'Oh, thank goodness for that!' said Winnie. 'I prefer our old scruffy house, too. And old scruffy me and you.'

She waved her wand. 'Abracadabra!'
Instantly they were back to scruffy normal.

'I'll make us a maggot and carrot-mould milkshake with what's in the fridge, shall I?' said Winnie. And she threw away the tin of Fogle's Fancy Nancy Food for Faddy Cats, golden paw print and all, and slammed the bin lid shut.

WINNIE'S
Alien Sleepover

'All those millions and squillions of stars and planets!' said Winnie, gazing through her telescope. 'They're as twinkly as glow-worms needing the loo! Do you think there are cats and witches on any of those twinkly places, Wilbur?'

'Meow,' Wilbur shrugged.

Just then—**bloopety-bleep-bloop!**

'Who the frilly bloomers is calling me at this time of night?' wondered Winnie.

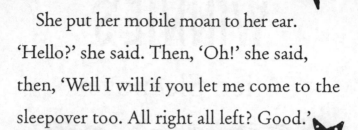

She put her mobile moan to her ear.
'Hello?' she said. Then, 'Oh!' she said,
then, 'Well I will if you let me come to the
sleepover too. All right all left? Good.'

'Meeow?' asked Wilbur.

'We're going to a star-watching
sleepover at the school. The head teacher's
mad about stars, and they want to use our
telescope.'

Winnie packed her old sleeping bag, her
nightie, her Beddy-Teddy, her hairnet,
her slip-sloppers and her toothbrush. She
added her vulture-feather pillow.

'In case we have a pillow fight,' she
told Wilbur. 'But mostly we have to be
looking out of the window for a fiery-
tailed comet that only comes this way once

76

every thirteen hundred years. Hmm. Some
snackaroos for a midnight feast would
be a good idea.' Winnie waved her wand.
'Abracadabra!'

And instantly there were some Sun buns
made from top hot chillies, beetroot and
pongberries. Some Earth fudge made from
real earth that still had some tasty morsels
of ants and worms in it. And some Moon
meringues, made from alligator egg whites
and minced maggots to give them a nice
cratery appearance.

'Box them up, Wilbur, and we must be on our way.'

It was a wobbly broom ride with all that luggage, but it wasn't far to the school.

The little ordinaries were ever so excited about the sleepover. The head teacher was ever so excited about the comet.

'I'm ever so excited too!' said Winnie.

She picked up her pillow and walloped
a couple of little ordinaries with it,
showering feathers everywhere.

'Ow!' protested the little ordinaries.

Mrs Parmar and Wilbur put their heads
in their hands and paws.

As the sky grew darker outside, things
quietened down inside. The only one still
jumping around was the head teacher.

80

'I can't see anything twinkling!' he said.
'Why isn't the comet in the sky?'

'Let me have a look,' said Winnie. She
peered through the telescope, and, 'Ooh,
I've found a whole new planet!' she said.
'Urrgh, it's a horrible looking place. It's
a dirty white colour with a toady sort of
green middle. Oh! Now it's gone!'

'That was my eyeball, you silly old witch!' said the head teacher. 'I was just looking to see if anything was blocking the lens.'

'Well something was blocking it!' said Winnie. '*You!*'

'What a useless silly old telescope!' said the head teacher.

'You're a useless silly old head teacher!' said Winnie.

82

'Now stop that, both of you!' said Mrs Parmar. 'You're over-tired, and it's making you both crotchety. The sky is cloudy, so nobody is going to see anything. What we all need is some sleep!'

'But my comet . . .' wailed the head teacher.

'I want to look through the telescope!' shouted a little ordinary. 'He hasn't let anyone else have a go yet!'

'Who'd like some of my midnight feast to cheer us all up?' said Winnie.

'Noo!' wailed the little ordinaries.

'Well then, I've got another idea,' said Winnie. 'Each of you, take a piece of paper, and roll it up to make your own telescope. Then we'll all do a countdown before looking out of the window.'

So everyone rolled paper telescopes, and began to count down, 'Ten! Nine! Eight! . . .'

Meanwhile Winnie nipped outside and got on her broom.

'I wouldn't recommend coming for this ride, Wilbur!' she said. Winnie waved her wand. *Abracadabra!*'

85

Zoom! Off shot Winnie on her broom, up into the cloudy night sky, her broom bristles ablaze with firework flames and sparkles and smoke and bangs!

'... Three! Two! One! ... Ooh!' said the little ordinaries, gazing through their telescopes.

'Hooray!' shouted the head teacher. 'My lovely comet at last! I've seen it! I can put a tick in my *I Spy the Sky* book!'

So everyone was happy. And everyone was tired. By the time Winnie got back into the school hall, they were all asleep.

But Winnie felt all fizzed up by her fiery ride through the sky. She looked through her telescope. The cloud was beginning to clear . . .

'I can see something!' said Winnie. 'It looks like a flying woodlouse, but, ooh, it's getting bigger! It's getting closer!'

Now the strange thing was so close that Winnie could see a sort of window in its side, and there was something a bit like a telescope sticking out of the window.

'Whatever the biggle-boggle is that?' said Winnie. But—**snoorrre**—was the

only reply she got from the school hall.

CRUMP!

'It's landed in the playground!' said
Winnie and she rushed outside, just in
time to see something coming out of the
flying woodlouse.

'Er, hello!' said Winnie. 'Welcome to
Earth. Do you like fudge?'

'**Piff**,' said the whatever-it-was.

'Where are you from, if you don't mind me asking?' said Winnie.

'**Snid-peep-lug**,' said the whatever-it-was.

So Winnie held out the head teacher's *I Spy the Sky* book, and the whatever-it-was pointed at Mars.

'You're a Martian!' said Winnie. 'Ooh,
would you write something in Martian in
the head teacher's special book? He'll be
as thrilled as a naked mole rat that's just
found a petticoat if you do!'

It turned out that the Martian was nosy, just like the head teacher. It looked through the window into the school and made notes in a Martian sort of notebook. It wrote squiggles that said in Martian that Earth beings live in bags on floors, and make 'snore' sounds. It noted that some have furry faces and whiskers.

The Martian tried Winnie's Moon meringues, and it squiggled 'urgh' in Martian in its notebook.

Winnie waved the Martian goodbye, just as the sun was coming up.

Then she got in her sleeping bag and went to sleep.

When everyone woke up for breakfast,
Winnie told Mrs Parmar and the little
ordinaries and the head teacher about her
Martian friend.

'Oh, Winnie!' declared Mrs Parmar. 'It
must have been a dream.'

'It was as real as the wart on your nose!'
said Winnie indignantly.

'Look! It even wrote in the *I Spy the Sky* book!'

'My book is ruined!' wailed the head teacher, and he tried to rub out the squiggles.

'Meeow,' said Wilbur. Luckily only Winnie understood what he meant by that: 'What a silly as a frilly-billy man the head teacher is!'

Enjoy more magic moments with **Winnie AND Wilbur**